READY, SET, 100TH DAY!

Written and illustrated by **Nancy Elizabeth Wallace**

Marshall Cavendish Children

Special thanks to Kate Fleming, Patti Darragh, Janice DeAngelo,
Dorothy Greco, Deb Verrillo,
and always to Margery, Anahid, and Virginia

Text and illustrations copyright © 2011 by Nancy Elizabeth Wallace
Marshall Cavendish Corporation, 99 White Plains Road, Tarrytown, NY 10591
www.marshallcavendish.us/kids

Library of Congress Cataloging-in-Publication Data

Wallace, Nancy Elizabeth.
Ready! Set! 100th day! / written and illustrated by Nancy Elizabeth
Wallace. — 1st Marshall Cavendish ed.
p. cm.
Summary: Minna's family pitches in to help her come up with the perfect
project for the hundredth day of school, from twenty sets of five sticks to
two sets of fifty pieces of pasta.
ISBN 978-0-7614-5956-9 (hardcover) — ISBN 978-0-7614-6070-1 (ebook)
[1. Set theory—Fiction. 2. Hundred (The number)—Fiction. 3. Hundredth Day
of School—Fiction. 4. Family life—Fiction.] I. Title. II. Title: Ready!
Set! one hundredth day!
PZ7.W15875Rds 2011   [E]—dc22   2011001128

The illustrations are rendered in paper, photographs, and colored pencils.
Book design by Virginia Pope
Editor: Margery Cuyler

Printed in China (E)
First edition
1 3 5 6 4 2

To the Buerkle Family:
Brian, Stacey, Ava, and Lia,
with love and thanks
N.E.W.

One Sunday morning, Minna sat on the living-room floor arranging sticks. "Five, ten, fifteen, twenty."

"Why are you saying five, ten, fifteen, twenty, Minna?" asked Pip.

"I'm making sets of fives," said Minna. "The one-hundredth day of school is this week. I'm trying to think of a really, really different idea for my Ready! Set! One Hundred! project."

"Can I do fives, too?" asked Pip.

"Sure."

Pip helped Minna tally the sticks. When they had twenty groups, Minna counted.

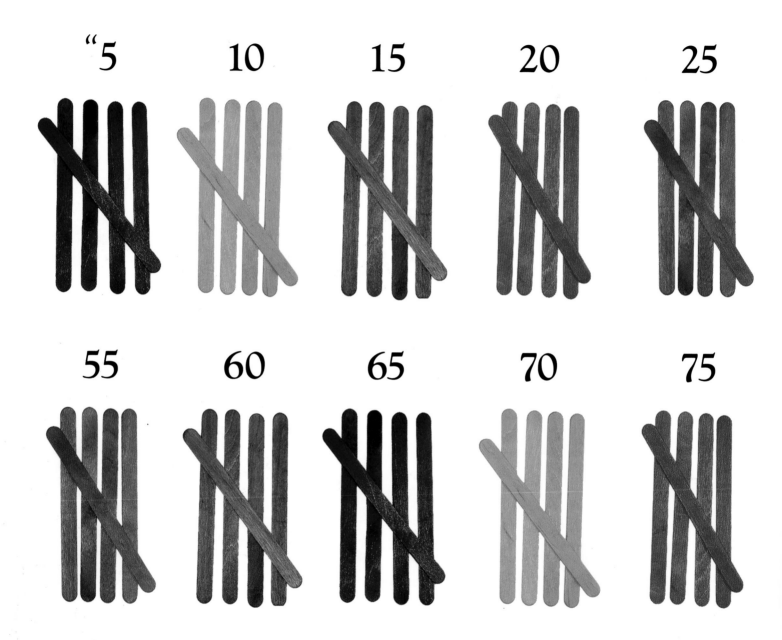

"5   10   15   20   25

55   60   65   70   75

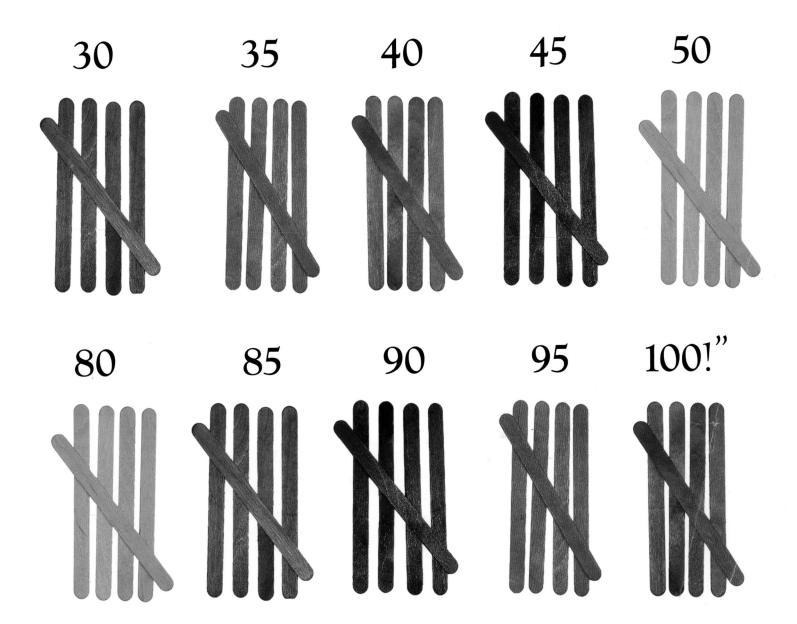

30 35 40 45 50

80 85 90 95 100!"

"One hundred is a lot," said Pip.
"Let's stack the sticks," said Minna.

"Like this."

They added more and more
sticks until they had a tower.
    "We're super stick-stackers,"
said Minna.

"Let's crash it down," said Pip.

Minna swept the sticks back into the blue bag.

"The sets of sticks are a good idea for your one-hundredth-day project," said Mom.

"Sticks are fun, but," said Minna, "I'm still thinking."

"If you need any help, let us know," said Dad.

"Tens. . . . What can I do for tens?" Minna said to herself.

Minna roamed around her room.
She looked on her bed.

She looked in her basket of bows.

She stopped at her art shelves.
She had an idea.
She got her green box and
colored paper.

"Dad!" Minna called. "Would you
help me, please? With the tens?"

Dad went into her room. "Hmmmm. Ten punches and ten pieces of colored paper."

Minna and Dad each picked a paper punch to start.

"Ready! SET! Go!" said Minna.

They laughed. The paper punches *click, click, clicked*.

They put the shapes in lines. Minna counted.

"10
20
30
40
50
60
70
80
90
100!"

Then . . .

Minna slid the shapes around on the big piece of yellow paper.

"That looks really nice," said Dad. "The shape sets are a great idea for your one-hundredth-day project."

"I like shapes, but," said Minna, "I'm still thinking."

Minna slipped the shapes into an envelope. "Twenties next, that's easy."

Minna got her purple polka-dot pouch.
"Pip. Want to help?"

They placed the pom-poms in rows.
Minna counted.

"20
40
60
80
100!"

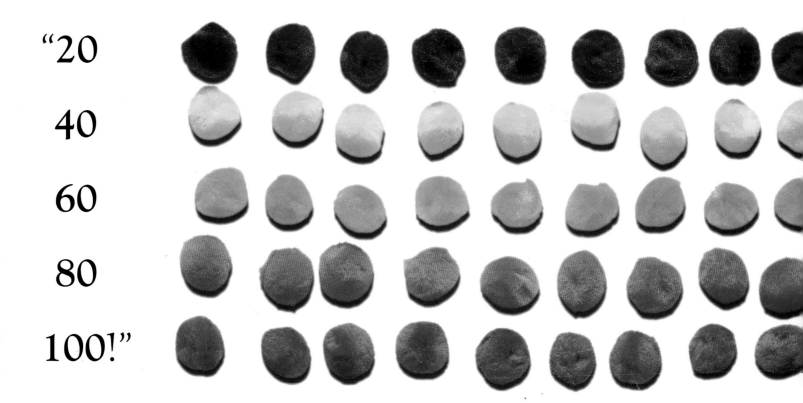

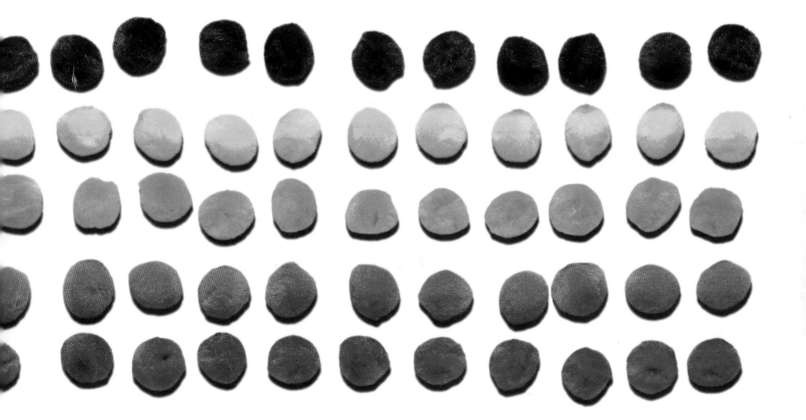

Then . . .

They picked out pom-poms and made a pattern.

"Look, Minna!" said Pip. "We made a pom-pom caterpillar! Pom-poms are good sets."

"The colors are nice and bright. But," she said, "I'm still thinking." They gathered the pom-poms and put them back in the pouch.

"25."

"25."

"25."

"Mom! Would you help me with twenty-five?"

"Let's look in my desk," called Mom. "Maybe that will give you some ideas."

Mom opened the desk drawer. "Pencils, pens, erasers, stamps, a big box of paper clips, tape, scissors."

"Paper clips!" said Minna. "Perfect!"

Mom helped her group the paper clips.

Minna counted.

"25   50   75   100!"

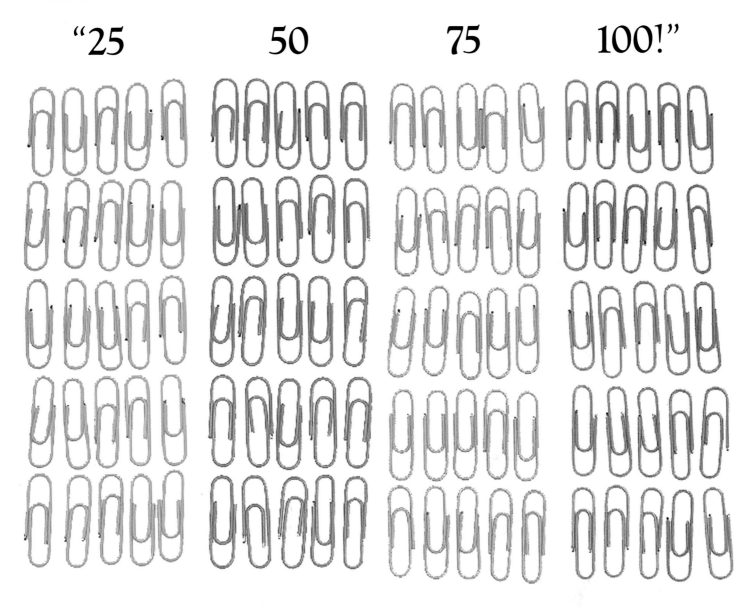

Then . . .

Minna wrote:

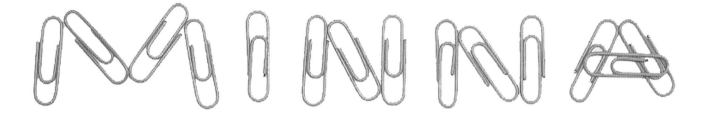

Mom smiled. She wrote:

"Wouldn't the paper clips work for your Ready! Set! One Hundred! project?" asked Mom.

"Paper clips are different, but," said Minna, "I'm still thinking!"

They scooped up the paper clips and put them back in the box.

"Almost time for lunch," said Dad. "We've got some bow and some wheel pasta."

"Dad! Wait!" said Minna.

"I can use pasta!"

Mom and Pip helped Minna count out fifty bows and fifty wheels on the kitchen table.

"50

100!"

said Minna. "I like the rows of wheels and bows, but I'm still thinking."

They slid the pasta into the box and set the table.

They had salad and bread for lunch.

"Yum," said Pip.

Minna whispered to herself, "Fives, tens, twenties . . ."

"Are you still thinking, Minna?" asked Pip.

Minna nodded.

"Sticks or shapes, paper clips, pom-poms or pasta—any of those sets are terrific," said Mom.

Minna looked at Mom. Suddenly she knew what she wanted to do.

After lunch, Minna gathered the green envelope, the yellow box,
the blue bag, the purple polka-dot pouch,
pasta, paper, and her glue stick.
She got to work.

When her project was finished, she showed Mom, Dad, and Pip.
They clapped.
"You are ready!" said Mom.
"Set!" said Dad.
"One hundred!" said Pip.

At school the next day, it was Minna's turn to share. She said, "I made a picture! I chose ten sets of ten."

"What a fun one-hundredth-day idea!" said Mrs. Bloom.

"Cool!" said Tyrone.

Happy
100th Day
of School

Then Minna asked,
"Can you find all
ten sets of ten?
Ready! SET! . . .

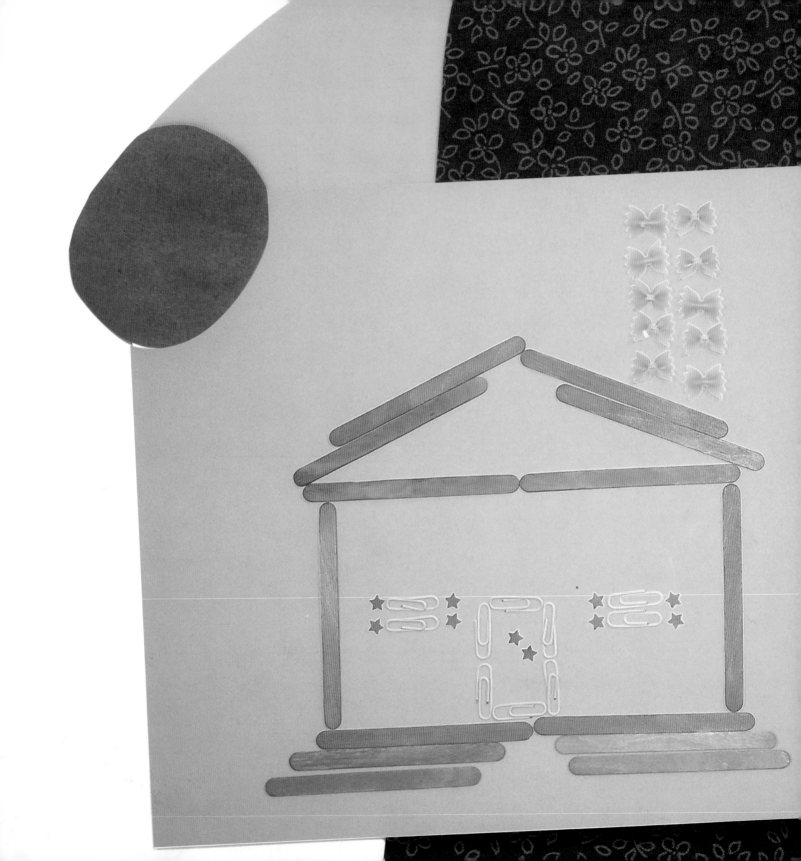

100!"

Did YOU find?

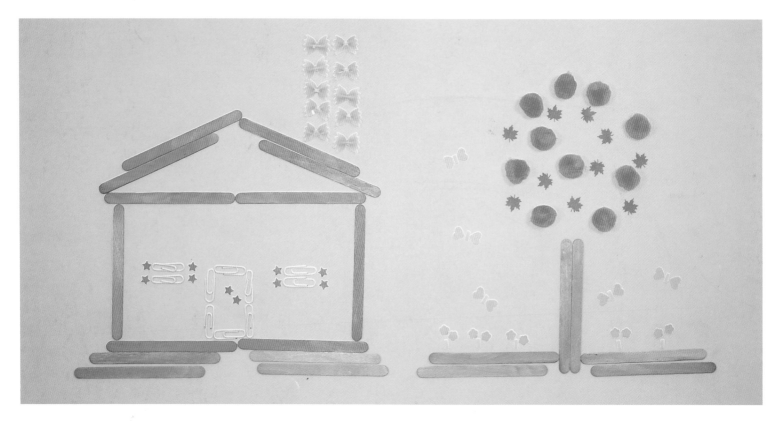

10 red sticks
10 pasta bows
10 flowers
10 leaves
10 pom poms
10 paper clips
10 stars
10 rectangles
10 hearts
10 green sticks

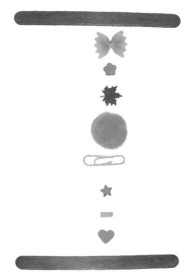

SETS!

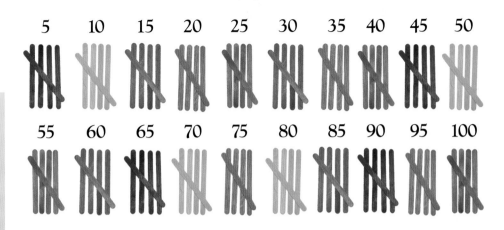

| 5 | 10 | 15 | 20 | 25 | 30 | 35 | 40 | 45 | 50 |

| 55 | 60 | 65 | 70 | 75 | 80 | 85 | 90 | 95 | 100 |

10
20
30
40
50
60
70
80
90
100

20
40
60
80
100

| 25 | 50 | 75 | 100 |

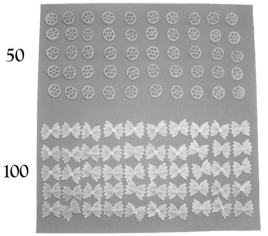

50

100

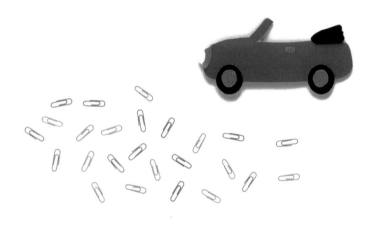